Kay Thompson's

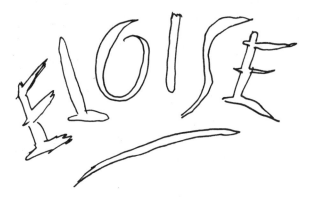

Drawings by Hilary Knight

A book for precocious grown-ups

PUFFIN BOOKS

Puffin Books, Penguin Books Ltd, Harmondsworth, Middlesex, England
Viking Penguin Inc., 40 West 23rd Street, New York, New York 10010, U.S.A.
Penguin Books Australia Ltd, Ringwood, Victoria, Australia
Penguin Books Canada Ltd, 2801 John Street, Markham, Ontario, Canada L3R 1B4
Penguin Books (N.Z.) Ltd, 182–190 Wairau Road, Auckland 10, New Zealand

First published in the U.S.A. by Simon & Schuster Inc. 1955
Published in Puffin Books 1985

Made and printed in Great Britain by
William Clowes Ltd
Filmset in Plantin Light

I am Eloise

I am six

I am a city child
I live at The Plaza

There is a lobby which is enormously large
with marble pillars and ladies in it and a revolving
door with 𝒫𝒫 on it

I spend an awful lot of time in the lobby

For instance every day I have to go to

Reception and see what's happening there

Then I stop by the Desk to see if they have
any stamps

Then I go to the phones
and make several calls to see
if anybody's in

The man in charge knows who I am

If there is a lot of luggage trying to get in the elevator and these people are all in a crowd and smoking and from out of town or something, I edge into the middle of it and lose my skate key

I am a nuisance in the lobby

Mr Salomone said so

He is the Manager

I always say "Good morning, Mr Salomone"

and he always says "Good morning, Eloise"

My mother knows The Owner

I live on the top floor
Of course I am apt to be on any floor at any time
And if I want to go anywhere I simply take the
elevator

For instance if I happen to be on the second floor I just press that button until it comes up and as soon as that door is open I get in and say *"5th floor* please" and when those doors clank shut we ride up and I get out on the *5th floor* and as soon as that elevator is out of sight I skibble up those stairs to the *8th floor* and then I press that button and when that same elevator comes up and as soon as that door is open I get in and say *"15th floor* please" and then when those doors clank shut we ride up and I get out on the *15th floor* and as soon as that elevator is out of sight I skibble down to the *12th floor* and press that button and when that same elevator comes up and those doors open I say *"The Lobby* please" and then those doors clank shut and we ride down without saying absolutely one word and then I get into the next elevator and go all the way up.

Then I get off at the top floor
And look in the mirror at me

ELOISE

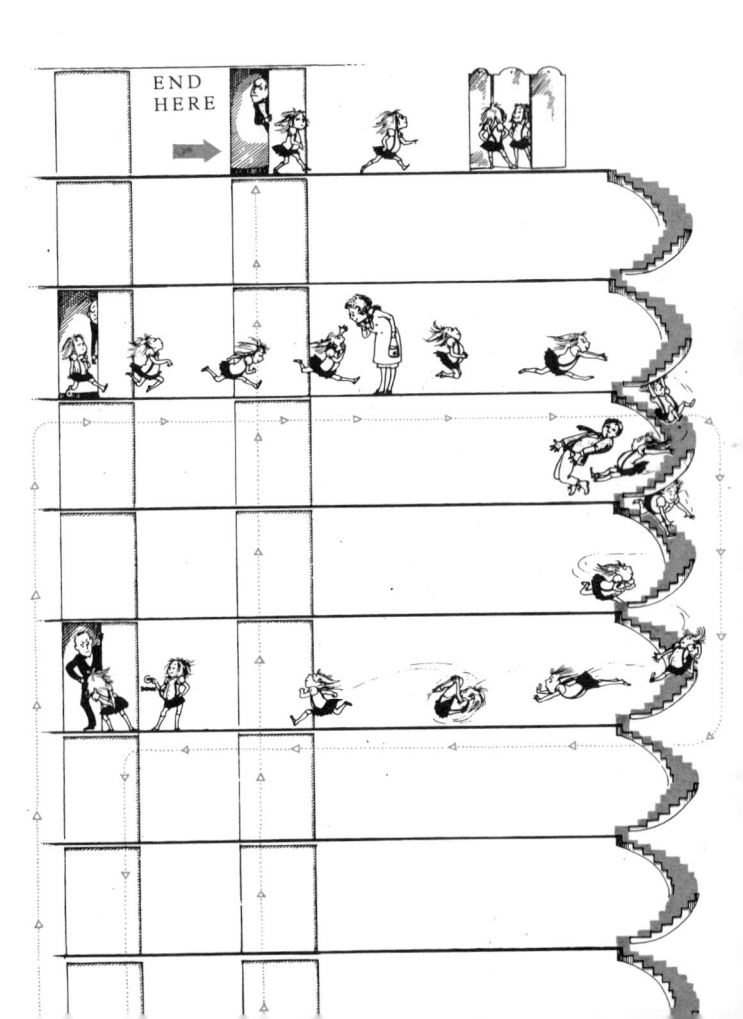

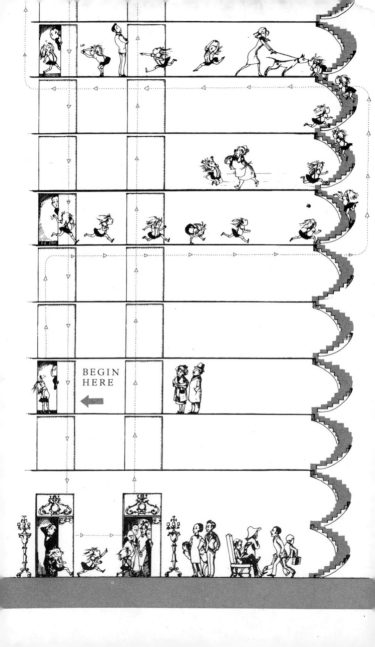

BEGIN
HERE

I live down at the end of the hall

Sometimes I take two sticks and skidder them along the walls

And when I run down the hall I slomp my feet against the woodwork which is very good for scuffing and noise

Sometimes I slomp my skates if I want to make a really loud and terrible racket

We have a buzzer on our front door
I always lean on it
That's how Nanny knows it's me
ELOISE

Nanny is my nurse
She wears tissue paper in her dress
and you can hear it
She is English and has 8 hairpins
made out of bones
She says that's all she needs in
this life for Lord's sake

Nanny says she
would rawther I didn't
talk talk talk all the time
She always says
everything 3 times
like Eloise you
cawn't cawn't cawn't
Sometimes I hit her
on the ankle with a tassel
She is my mostly companion

It has a coat rack which is as large as me

I have a dog that looks like a cat

His name is Weenie

Sometimes I put sunglasses on him

Then I have to scratch his back with a wire hanger

I have a turtle
His name is Skipperdee

He eats raisins and wears sneakers

The Plaza is the only hotel in New York
that will allow you to have a turtle

Skipperdee and me we always know it's morning
because Weenie breathes in our face and kisses us

The absolutely first thing I have to do
is plait Skipperdee's ears
Otherwise he gets cross and develops a rash

Nanny gets up feeling tired tired tired

and puts on her kimono

and skibbles over to slam those

windows down shut so that we don't

freeze freeze freeze

Then she stretches her muscles
and feels fresh fresh fresh

Nanny yawns out loud

Then I pick up the telephone
and call Room Service

Ooooooooo I absolutely love Room Service
They always know it's me
and they say "Yes, Eloise?"
And I always say "Hello, this is me E L O I S E
and would you kindly send one roast-beef bone,
one raisin and seven spoons to the top floor and
charge it please
Thank you very much"

Then I hang up and look at the ceiling for a while
and think of a way to get a present

I usually yawn out loud several times

Then Nanny gives the signal and Weenie and
Skipperdee and me we skibble out of bed as fast as
everly we can and Nanny wraps us in our robe and
holds us tight
And I pat her on her botto
which is large

Then we have to do our morning duties and laugh and sing

London from bottom to top is zup
The keeper in the shop is zup
And even Mrs Mop is zup
Oh what a love-a-ly mawning

In Trafalgar Square the Bobby's zup
In Piccadilly the Nippy's zup
In Covent Garden the Clippy's zup
Oh what a love-a-ly mawning

We're zup and we've got to be jolly clean
From head to toe and in between
Zup good morning and how've ya been
Oh what a love-a-ly mawning

The Royal Navy is up-is-zup
Buckingham Palace is up-is-zup
And even the BBC is-zup
Oh what a love-a-ly
Oh what a love-a-ly
Oh what a love-a-ly mawning

The Roy-al Na-vy is up-is-zup   Buck-ing-ham Pal-ac

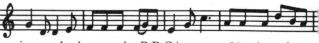

up-is-zup And e-ven the B B C is-zup   Oh what a love-a

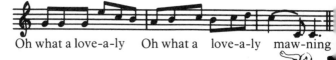

Oh what a love-a-ly   Oh what a   love-a-ly   maw-ning

Oooooooooo I just love Nanny I absolutely do

While I'm brushing my teeth
there is this pigeon who is always
hanging around our bathroom window
and he does absolutely nothing but coo
He is fat and grisly and I yell at him and he
flies over to the Sherry-Netherland Hotel for
a while to see what they're up to

Weenie and me weigh 36 pounds
Nanny weighs 18 stones

Skipperdee weighs absolutely nothing at all
unless he has his sneakers on
Then of course he weighs ½ a pound

Then Nanny puts on her corset which is
enormously large but which is very good for her
back

Kleenex makes a very good hat

When we are clean we skibble in our scuffs to the kitchen
and there is René with Room Service

René always says "Bonjour, Eloise, voici votre petit déjeuner"
Nanny always says "My my my doesn't that look good!"
And I always say "Bonjour, René, merci and charge it please"

Nanny has Irish bacon
which reminds her of her brother
You have to eat oatmeal or
you'll dry up
Anybody knows that
Nanny likes her coffee hot hot hot

An egg cup makes a very good hat

I have two dolls which is enough
Their names are Sabine and Saylor
Sabine is a rag doll and she has absolutely
no face at all partially because she came from
Jamaica by Air Express
Otherwise she has shoe-button eyes and
two right legs
She is *rawther* unusual

Saylor is a very large doll and has a hard head
and no arms
She was in the most terriblest accident and she
bleeded so hard she almost choked in the night
and this ambulance came and took her to this
hospital and it was an emergency and they had to
give her all this terribly dark medicine and a lot of
Band-aids and when she came back home she was
weak weak weak and had to take cod-liver oil
I gave her a strawberry leaf from under my
grapefruit for not whimpering and Weenie
licked her face
They have to have a teaspoon of water
every hour or so, so you can see they are an
extremely lot of extra work

Here's what I like to do
Make things up

Here's what I hate
Peter Rabbit

Here's what I can do

Chew gum

Write

Spell

Stand on my head for the longest amount of time

Stand on my toes

Get dizzy and fall down

Make a terrible face

And here's the thing of it

Most of the time I'm on the telephone

My day is rawther full
I have to call the Valet and tell him
to get up here and pick up
my sneakers to be cleaned and pressed
and have them back
for sure without fail

Then I have to play the piano and
look in the mirror for a while

Then I have to open and close the door for
a while and as soon as I hear talking and laughing
I skidder out and run down the hall

and if there is an open door I have
to walk in and pretend I am an orphan
and sometimes I limp and sort of bend
to the side and look sort of
sad in between the arms
and they give me a piece of
melon or something

Then I roam around the halls

Then I have to scurry down to
the 10th floor to adjust those
thermostats in case anyone needs it

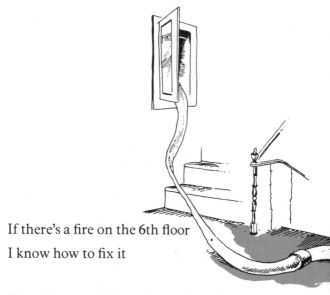

If there's a fire on the 6th floor
I know how to fix it

Then I have to hide and see what those
Hotel Officers are up to
All they do is walk and talk
I have never been arrested

Then I have to hurry back to the top floor

Our day maid's name is Johanna
She has earrings with garnets
and is going to take her Social Security
to Bavaria on her birthday
One time she saw this man in this hair net
and he bawled her out for taking his razor blades
I have to help her put on those
pillowcases or she'll never be through
by 4 for Lord's sake
She has to be through by 4

Then I have to go around to that Service Elevator
on the 6th floor and see what everybody's
thrown away and if I want it or not, like ribbon
or something like that

Then I have to go down to help the Switchboard Operators in case there are any DAs and there has to be some sort of message taken or something like that

If there is an Exit sign I always have to go into it
because there might be a mattress in there
and I can lie down on it and get some rest so I can
carry on for Lord's sake

Oh my Lord I am absolutely so busy
I don't know how I can possibly
get everything done

Then I have to hop around for a while

I have lunch at the Palm Court if it is too rainy
and see Thomas
We are both rawther fond of talking and he gives
me Gugelhopfen
Thomas has a son in the Marines who got married
on a shoestring
Thomas has a Porsche

I always go in the Persian Room after 4
to see my friend Bill
He is a busboy in the night and
goes to school in the day and
his eyes water
Here's where he's been
Madrid
Here's where I've been
Boiler Room

Then I scamper to the Terrace Room
where those débutantes are prancing around

Then I have to skibble into the Baroque Room
because sometimes there is this chalk and there is
this pitcher with ice water in it and you should see
the cigar smoke left over from a General Motors
meeting
Oh my Lord

Then I have to help the busboys and waiters get
set up in the Crystal Room
They always wait until the last second for Lord's
sake and then we have to rush our feet off

I go to all the weddings in the
White and Gold Room
and I usually stay for the reception

There are absolutely nothing but rooms in the
Plaza

Sometimes if they are having
this enormous affair in the
Grand Ballroom I get there early
to help Joe set up the lights in the
ceiling and before anybody
gets there we just scamper up this ladder and hide
up there in those holes
Oh my Lord is it ever swelteringly hot up there
I always wear my sun visor

I am all over the hotel
Half the time I am lost

But mostly I am on the first floor because
that's where Catering is
So I have to go down there every day for at least
three hours and sometimes I have to go at night
Oh my Lord do they ever have a lot of things
going on down there

Altogether I have been to 56 affairs including
Halloween

There is this Oak Room which is to the right
if you want to have a broken mint or
something like that

And you have to go downstairs
to the Rendezvous Room which is
very good for hiding over a long
period of time and for doing a tour jeté or so

The Package Room has all these packages in it and
sometimes I have to help them lift those heavy
boxes and look for small packages that might be
for me ELOISE

Sometimes I go into the Men's Room which is very good for playing Railroad Station or something like that

Every Wednesday I have to go to the Barber Shop
and have Vincent shape my hair
He does absolutely nothing but talk and swiggles
me around in that chair and hurts my neck with
that brush
Sometimes I sklonk him in the kneecap

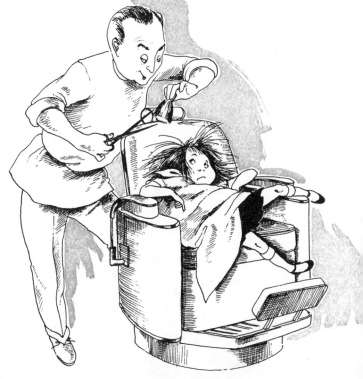

Vincent says that if I am not careful I am not
going to have a hair on my head by the time I'm 7
for Lord's sake

Getting bored is not allowed
Sometimes I comb
my hair with a fork

Sometimes I wear my arm in a sling

Sometimes I put a rubber band
on the end of my nose

Toe shoes make very good ears
Sometimes I wear them to lunch

Here's what I like to do
Pretend

Sometimes I am a mother with 40 children

Sometimes I am a giant with fire coming out of
my hair

Sometimes I get terribly sick and have to be
waited on

Sometimes I get so sick my head falls over and is
wobbling until it is loose
Then we have to call my mother long distance and
charge it
My mother is 30 and has a charge account at
Cartier's

She wears a 3½ shoe

I put a large cabbage leaf on my head
when I have a headache
It makes a very good hat

She goes to Europe and to Paris
and sends for me if there's some sun
I am always packed in case I have to leave on
T W A at a moment's notice or something like that
My mother has I B M stock and she knows an
ad man whatever that is

Sometimes my mother goes to Virginia
with her lawyer
He has an office on Madison Avenue
He has already had the whooping cough
and the measles
Sometimes I give him rubber candy
He is absolutely so dumb he eats it
Sometimes he brings me a present
whether I deserve it or not
I usually do

Here's what he likes
Martinis
Here's what I like
Dandelions

Sometimes I have a temper fit

But not very often

I absolutely dislike school
so Philip is my tutor
He goes to Andover
My mother knows the Dean

He wears red garters and is boring boring boring

When we have our French lesson he reads in
French about la petite cousine de Marie and
her jardin and sometimes I listen to him but
not very often

Here's what makes Philip angry

He says "Alors! nous commencerons" and I say

"Alors! nous commencerons"

And he says "Shall we settle down Eloise?"

And I say "Shall we settle down Eloise?"

And he says "That's quite enough Eloise"

And I say "That's quite enough Eloise"

And he says "I mean it Eloise"

And I say "I mean it Eloise" right back at him

And he looks at me with fiercely eyes

And I look right back at him with fiercely eyes

And then he says "That will do Eloise"

And then I say "That will do Eloise"

And then he shouts "Eloise I mean it"

And then I shout "Eloise I mean it" right after him

And then he gets madder and says "Stop it at once Eloise"

And then I say "Stop it at once Eloise"

And then he stands up and says "Very well Eloise"
And then I stand up and say "Very well Eloise"
And then he walks around the room
And then I walk around the room

And then he screams "Nanny"
Then I scream "Nanny"
And Nanny comes in yelling "Non non non
Eloise" and she claps her hands and Skipperdee
and me we skibble over and hide behind the
television or fall dead behind a hidden door

And then Nanny puts her arm around Philip
and calls Room Service and says "Send three of
everything please"

And when the waiter brings the check Nanny
signs my mother's name
And I simply tell him to "charge it please and
thank you very much"
Then I do a cartwheel

Philip is always glad to go home

Every night I have to call Room Service
to send up that menu so we can order
our dinner for Lord's sake
I always have to read it for a few seconds or so
Then I just say "I'll have the Planked Medallion of
Beef Tenderloin with Fresh Vegetables Maison
please and two raisins, one strawberry leaf and one
clams in season s'il vous plaît and charge it please
Thank you very much"

Oooooooooooooooooo I absolutely love Room
Service

The night maid's name is Lily

She married the engineer of the subway and

' cut her hair but I think she's sorry

She gives us extra pillowcases and soap

Once there was this most terriblest storm that
came up and it rained and all this thunder was
clomping itself into this water and all these people
were drowning without air
Absolutely no one was saved

Paper cups are very good for talking to Mars

T V is in the Drawing Room

I always watch it with my parasol in case there's some sort of glare

And oh my Lord when it's fight night Nanny is absolutely wild and we have to scamper into our places and get ready and Nanny has to find her Players and I have to get my binoculars and call Room Service and order three Pilsener Beers for Nanny and one meringue glacée for me E L O I S E and charge it please

Thank you very much

Oooooooooooooooooooo I absolutely love T V

Every night when it's time to go to bed Nanny
yawns out loud and says she is tired tired tired
I make as much noise as I possibly can like turning
on the record player very loud and howling a lot

Then I have to brush Nanny's hair
for her And then we both yawn out
loud and get into our
pajamas

Then I have to put on my Don't Disturb sign
and get Skipperdee and Weenie and me all tucked
in and then Nanny opens the windows
enormously wide so we can have air air air
Then she turns out the light

Nanny has a mole

Sometimes we go to sleep right away
But not very often
Sometimes Weenie and Skipperdee and me we get
out of bed and go into that closet and look around
for a while and when we get in there there is this
cave and it is so dark in there that it's absolutely
black and there is this big bug in there that has
those enormously large feathers and he picks us up
by our necks and sklanks us around in his paws
and carries us down into this deep well that is all
filled with tigers and lions and birds of prey and
they eat us up raw and step on us and stamp their

feet on us and absolutely rank us and we have to
run for our lives and drag each other on our
stomach and scrape our face along the side until
we are absolutely breathing and stretching our
arms to reach that closet door barely in time and
our heart is beating and we have to wake Nanny
with a flashlight in her face to save us and put
witch hazel and cotton on all of our toenails

And Nanny has to get up and pamper me and spoil me for a while while I am out of my head with fever and pain

After all I am only 6

Oh my Lord
There's so much to do
Tomorrow I think I'll pour a pitcher of water
down the mail chute

Oooooooooooooooooooo I absolutely love the Plaza!